The **FIDORI TRILOGY**

BOOK 2:
THE PURPLE FLOWER

BY JASMINE FOGWELL

destinēe *media*

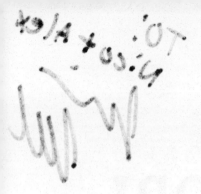

The Purple Flower
Book 2 of The Fidori Trilogy
Jasmine Fogwell
© Copyright 2016 By Jasmine Fogwell

Published by Destinée Media: www.destineemedia.com
Written by Jasmine Fogwell: www.jasminefogwell.com
Illustrations and cover illustration by Amanda Kramer Kaczynski
Interior design by Julie Lundy: www.juliekaren.com
Cover design by Devon Brown: www.oxburger.wix.com/oxburger

ISBN: 978-1-938367-26-7

Dedication

This book is dedicated to Blake Allen. Together, we created the creatures called Fidoris and I could not have written this book without him.

Pronunciation Key

Some of the names in this book have been inspired by my time in a small village in the Swiss Alps. Pronounce them as you wish, but this is how they sound when I tell the story!

Rionzi: RYE-on-zee

DuCret: DEW-cray

Nemesté: NEM-es-tay

Fidoris: fi-door-ees

BE SURE TO READ ALL OF

The FIDORI TRILOGY

BOOK 1:
AN UNLIKELY FRIENDSHIP

BOOK 2:
THE PURPLE FLOWER

BOOK 3:
THE JOURNEY TO THE
TOP OF THE TREES

BOOK 2:
THE PURPLE
FLOWER

Rionzi Breaks the Rules

Saleem sat in the lobby of the inn, staring out towards the forest. He could only see darkness beyond the quaint streetlights. His thoughts wandered. Inside, he was torn. Rionzi DuCrét had a very strict curfew for her walk. In the forty years he and his father had been responsible for her, she had never even thought of disobeying the rules that governed her limited walk in the forest once every two weeks. The penalty for breaking this condition was banishment. Some of the more vocal village people threatened banishment even to Saleem, and he feared his neighbours' responses if anyone found out she had disappeared—but, on the other hand, he could be free of her if she simply didn't come back.

For a few brief minutes, this new sense of freedom felt good, but a part of him would deeply miss the old lady. Although they rarely spoke, her presence in the inn, which was a place of constant transition, was a comfort for him. He was fascinated by her, in a way—by her extreme old age, for one thing. Despite her bitter facade, she seemed to hold on to hope. He wasn't sure what she hoped for, but he could feel it when, on rare occasions, he would run into her.

Clouds had covered the sky, and lightning flashed in the distance. A storm was blowing in, bringing rain across the valley. Finally, Saleem spotted a shadow in the dim streetlight that could be none other than Rionzi DuCrét. The way she wobbled along with her cloak covering her face, hunched over but still full of strength, was very distinct.

Water dripped off her coat as she reached the front door. She stomped the mud off her worn old boots. There were holes all over them, and inside her socks were brown and wet. The door creaked as she pushed through. The sound of rain splashing on the pavement grew as she entered. She closed the door quietly behind her, wiped her feet again, and hobbled towards the stairs. Each step creaked as she made her way up. Saleem sat beside the window and watched as she passed. If she saw him there, she didn't acknowledge it. He couldn't figure out why, but she looked more worn than usual. It could have been that she'd been out hours longer, but Saleem sensed it was more. Something was bothering her. He made his way to bed and fell asleep to wandering thoughts of what could be bothering the unique woman.

Alone in her quiet room on the third floor of the old inn, Rionzi DuCrét cried and then drifted off into a restless sleep.

At the other end of town, James was crying, as well. After Mrs. DuCrét accused him of lying about Zintar, James had run all the way back to his house and sat at the edge of the forest to finish crying before going inside. His mother noticed he was upset but didn't bother him too much about it, and James cried himself to sleep that night.

The week went by, and James was consumed with hatred for Rionzi DuCrét. It was a hatred brought on by confusion over their friendship. The shared experience of the Fidoris had created such a deep bond that he couldn't help but hate her. He was hurt, crushed, and the only way he could keep from crying all day was to be angry. Anger is a bit easier to handle than the pain of betrayal. At school, James was acting out, and at home he barely spoke. He took walks in the forest, kicking rocks, breaking sticks, and destroying the wildflowers. A few times, the pain was so fierce that anger couldn't even cover it, and he would lie down beside a tree, weeping.

During this same week, Rionzi DuCrét sat on her creaky balcony at the old inn, worried. She knew she had crushed her dearest friend. James was the only person in the world who understood her. She needed to talk to him. She needed to apologize for lashing out. She needed to beg him for forgiveness.

Rionzi had believed Zintar to be dead. After all these years, was it really possible that he was alive? She needed to see James again, but how? Would he speak to her? She tried to imagine herself in James's shoes. Would she talk to herself? Probably not, but she had to try. She could wait for him in the forest. He would come eventually, unless he was so crushed that even the forest brought no comfort. Her next walk wasn't until the following week, but she needed to see him before then. Perhaps she could sneak out in the darkness before dawn and return late into the night. It was possible nobody would notice. The thought of disobeying her contract was terrifying. She had never even considered it before, but it needed to be done. The truth of the Fidoris was too precious to be lost any longer. This was the best plan she could think of. Tomorrow was Saturday, and James would surely be out in the forest.

Rionzi DuCrét woke up at four a.m. It was still dark out. As she walked down the stairs, she was sure every guest would hear what, to her, sounded like elephants tramping through the building. But as she stepped out into the parking lot, she glanced back and noticed that no lights had come on. The thick dew of the morning sent a chill through the old lady. Rionzi put her scarf over her head and walked down through the sleeping Nemesté. Her footsteps echoed off the old cement houses. The fog wisped through the dim light given off by the streetlamps. Not a soul seemed to be awake at this hour, for which Rionzi was grateful. She reached the edge of the village and stood in the shadows, staring at James's house. Would he come out today?

Rionzi's withered old figure stood just behind a tree as the darkness turned to dusk and the sun began peeking up over the mountains. She decided she had better move deeper into the forest before the village awoke.

As the sun lit his room, James slowly came out of his restless dream. He lay awake, thinking. The

Fidoris came to mind, which wasn't uncommon for James these days. As usual, these thoughts brought a flood of mixed emotions. There was the ever-present sadness of the loss of his friend Zintar and the many fruitless walks he had taken to try to find him. Rionzi DuCrét came to mind, as well—the way she told wonderful stories of the Fidoris and the smile that lit up her face as she searched through her memories. But James's memories of her couldn't be separated from that day in the forest when she had yelled at him and accused him of lying. A few tears rolled down his cheeks. Finally, he decided to get up and head to the forest for the day. Despite all the confusion, it was still his favourite place to be.

Rionzi DuCrét lurked in the trees just off the thin, snakelike walking path, listening for the sound of footsteps. She had just dozed off for a minute in a sunbeam that broke through the canopy when she heard the familiar footsteps that could belong to none other than her friend James. They were quick, between a run and a walk, and

they were quiet and light as if he was moving on his tiptoes.

James skipped along into the forest, dodging the sunbeams in a sort of game. The farther he ventured, the more at home he felt. Without noticing her, he passed the tree where Rionzi DuCrét was sitting. As she stepped out onto the path, a twig snapped under her foot, and James heard the noise. Hoping it might be his Fidori friend, he turned around, and his gaze locked on Mrs. DuCrét. She looked back at him. They stood awkwardly like this for a moment, neither quite sure what to do.

Finally, Rionzi spoke. "James, please don't run away."

"You're not supposed to be here," James snarled as he tried to hold back the tears welling up inside him.

"I know," she said. "I took a great risk, but I needed to see you."

The tears came slowly. His voice was shaky as he tried to speak. "Why? You think I'm a liar."

Rionzi paused for a moment. She needed to think before she blurted out the wrong thing. She felt terrible as James stood, shaking, with tears streaming down his cheeks. He wanted an answer. That was why he couldn't run away.

"James, I know I shouldn't be here, but I needed to talk to you. Please hear me out." Rionzi hadn't had a serious talk with another human being in fifty years, and she was a bit out of practice. James was still standing there, so she continued talking. "I'm sorry I called you a liar. I've gone over and over our conversation in my mind, and I've come up with two conclusions. You see, James, I have never uttered the name Zintar. I thought you had somehow found out, or maybe, somehow, someone in Nemesté had heard and sent you to play an evil trick on me. Or perhaps Zintar is alive and he is the Fidori you met.

"I believed for fifty years that Zintar was dead and that I killed him, but if you're telling the truth, then that belief is false. For an ancient, stubborn old lady, I found it easier to believe you had lied than to untangle this belief. That was wrong, James. I was wrong. And what makes it worse is that I understand the pain and loneliness that has accompanied you, the pain of knowing something beautiful that no one else believes. I, of all people, shouldn't have left you alone. That's why I came today."

Throughout Rionzi's apology, James's tears had stopped, and a hint of a smile crossed his face. He turned away from her gaze and spoke. "Mrs. DuCrét, up until I met you, I was almost ready to accept that my friend wasn't real. I make up a lot of games, you know, and I was ready to believe Zintar was just a part of them—but you made me believe again that I did have a true friend."

There was a small pause, and both of them looked out through the trees.

"Come, James. Let's walk. I'll tell you about Zintar," Rionzi said.

There was no hesitation. The two headed off down the familiar path into the old forest. Rionzi hobbled along with her scarf over her head to keep from being recognized, and James scampered beside her, picking up old sticks and kicking rocks.

"As I've told you before, James," Rionzi began, "I lived on the trees with the Fidoris for nearly a year, although time is a funny thing up there. The sun rising and setting is all you need to know. Despite the Fidoris being creatures of habit, content with everything, they are really quite curious little things. They asked me for stories about my world. At first they thought I lived below the trees, down the beamers, and wondered how dark it must be, but I told them all about the shiny cities, where there weren't many trees, and the people who inhabited them. I explained to them about our houses and that we all sleep alone. At first I was worried that perhaps this would destroy some of the beauty of their innocence. However, they simply found it amusing and a bit odd.

"You know, I'm not sure they have longings quite the same as ours. Their curiosity doesn't seem to come about because they lack something. It's a genuine love of learning, a way to expand their imaginations or maybe just collect new ideas for their elaborate stories. They soak things up until they truly understand. I think they love their lives, though, from a human point of view, they may seem quite boring. I don't have an answer as to why they're so content, but my hunch is that it's because they truly understand love in relationships. We seem to have a longing for something that's absent, but they don't."

"Zintar was sad sometimes," James said. "He said he missed his family. He said he had never experienced such sadness before."

"I believe it," Rionzi said. She paused a moment, then asked, "James, did you know Zintar was a prince?"

"No! He didn't tell me that." James looked at Mrs. DuCrét, anxiously waiting to hear more about his friend with the big mushroom feet.

"Well, he is!" She loved the way James held on to every word she said about the Fidoris. "He was Motumbu's eldest son and was destined to become king someday. Zintar was one of the quieter Fidoris, but he loved listening to the stories. When they would gather around their campfire, Zintar would curl up and cuddle with a few other Fidoris, close his eyes, and immerse himself in the story. During the days, when we would be gathering sticks and trimming the trees, he would come up to me and want to know more details from my stories and the world of humans. Sometimes he would laugh at how silly some of our habits are, and other times he would cry because my stories were so sad.

"We spent a lot of time together, talking, laughing, and learning about each other. Zintar was different from his parents in that he was quieter and remained on the edge of the crowd, but it could be that because Motumbu and Aliumbra were king and queen, they had no choice but to be at the centre. I was told that King Motumbu used to be the same way."

"What do you mean?" James asked.

"He was once quiet and in the background, soaking up the stories of the elders. Zintar told me of a conversation he and his father once had. Zintar asked him, 'Do you think I'll make a good king someday?'

"His dad laughed a little and asked him a question in return: 'Do you think I am a good king?'

"'Of course,' Zintar said. 'All of us love you. You lead with kindness, you're not afraid, and you understand.'

"'If those are what you believe to be the qualities of a good king,' Motumbu answered, 'then I assure you, son, you will also be one.' There was a small pause in their conversation. Then Motumbu spoke again. 'Understanding is vital to overcoming fear,' he said. Zintar told me that single thought shaped who he was."

"Is that why people are afraid of you?" James blurted out. "Because they don't understand?"

Rionzi smiled at his question. "Yes, I suppose it probably is. I think we're afraid of what we don't understand. That's why people were afraid of our stories of the Fidoris. That's why I was afraid of what you said about Zintar. I couldn't understand how it was possible. The more we listen and understand something, the less scary it can be."

They wandered into a meadow, and the sun blinded them. The grass was tall, brushing against their legs. They could hear water trickling over the rocks at the far end of the clearing.

"We used to play in this field a lot," James recalled. "Zintar felt a bit more comfortable here because it was more open instead of enclosed by the trees."

Mrs. DuCrét asked, "What sort of things did you two do together?"

"Sometimes we would collect sticks and eat them. Well, I didn't, but he did. We would sort them into piles, and some would be salad, some would be rice, and some were our dessert. This was our favourite game. I tried to show him how to play soccer, but with his clumsy feet it wasn't very fun. We tried playing tag, but he couldn't run very fast. We built a fort once, and I remember having a hard time explaining houses to him."

"Oh, James," Rionzi said with some excitement, "that sounds wonderful."

As Rionzi and James continued walking through the meadow, unbeknownst to them, another creature lurked just past the trees. Simputus had been following them for some time. They were getting uncomfortably close to something she had hidden for nearly a year in a cave deep in the woods. It was guarded by the flowers, and she thought that was likely enough to scare them off—but she still followed just to be sure.

Her black eyes blended in with the shadows of the trees, and her light green feet kept her silent. She never imagined that after all these years, the old hag would return this far into the woods. The guilt of killing Zintar should have kept her away.

This curious boy, though…who was he? Simputus only remembered him as if from a dream. She hadn't actually been there when James picked her flowers, but when they started to work their evil, she had felt it and even caught a glimpse of his dying scraggly body. That scene of James on the forest floor, about to pass on to death, had been interrupted by a light so bright she'd had to close her eyes—and in that moment, the vision or dream, whatever it was, had vanished. Something must have happened in that moment, because here was that same boy, standing in front of her.

Suddenly, they both stopped. "James, can you feel that?" Rionzi said, looking around the field and staring into the shadows of the trees.

James didn't know what it was, but he felt it, too. "Yes, it's like one of my nightmares with those purple flowers," he said.

Rionzi DuCrét paused a minute, still scanning the forest for whatever was causing this strange sensation. "Perhaps we've wandered too far today, James."

James wasn't going to disagree with her. He didn't enjoy the fear that was taking over his body. He even looked down at his hands to make sure they weren't turning green like they had when he touched the purple flower. But there was a sense of something else, too. It was like a passing scent that vanished when he tried to focus on it or a vague memory that he could barely grasp. "Mrs. DuCrét, I'm scared, but maybe we're getting close to something important."

Rionzi felt it, too, but the fear was very strong. "No, James. I think we should go. She is near, I know it." Her eyes were wide open, bulging out of her wrinkly face. She grabbed James by the hand and began walking back across the field at a surprisingly fast pace for such an old lady.

In shock at being taken away so quickly, James was trying to regain his footing as they moved along. He kept looking behind them to the black opening on the other side of the field.

Simputus watched as they hastily walked away, thankful for the power she still held over them. She smiled a bit, but it was not a friendly smile.

Once they were far from the open field and that strange feeling was no longer with them, Rionzi let go of James's hand and sat on a large rock to catch her breath and compose herself. She had not been that afraid in a very long time.

James stumbled a bit when she let go of his hand. "What was that back there?" he asked.

Mrs. DuCrét's eyes were wide open. Her breathing was still very fast, though she tried to slow it down. She stared at James, thankful they were okay. As she sat there for another minute, she realized how tired she was. It had been a while since she'd moved that quickly. "James, I don't know what it was. There was something in that forest, and I cringe just thinking of how close to us it was."

"Do you think it was the lady with the purple flowers?" James asked.

"Yes," she answered. "I fear very much that she was there in the shadows. I know nothing else that could cause such fear in me. And you felt it, too, James."

"It was even scarier than when I picked those flowers and my body started turning green." He thought for a minute longer. "But I sensed something else, too, that was the opposite of scary, like that time I took a sip of the sweet sap Zintar gave me to bring me back to life."

Mrs. DuCrét looked puzzled. "No, it couldn't be. It had to be a nasty trick of Simputus," she said as she looked off into the distance.

"Couldn't be what?" James looked at her.

"Look, James, I don't know for certain, but I've only ever felt that feeling when I was with the Fidoris."

"Me, too, Mrs. DuCrét! Me, too!" he yelled with excitement. It was what he had been thinking, but he hadn't known how to say it.

There was a pause in their conversation. Rionzi DuCrét sat, still breathless, and James picked up a few pinecones and began throwing them in the air and trying to hit them with a stick like baseballs. What were these strange conflicting sensations that had come over each of them? They had both felt the presence of the wonderful creatures called Fidoris and the fear of that wretched creature called Simputus. The sensations had been stronger than in any of their dreams.

Suddenly, Mrs. DuCrét's eyes darted around. She was looking for something with urgency in her gaze. "James, we need to mark this spot."

He looked over at her. She had stood up and was collecting stones. "What are you doing?" he asked.

With fear in her voice, she said, "James, we need to come back here soon. We have to find out what this was." She had gathered enough rocks and began placing them in a pattern near the log she had been sitting on.

"What is it?" James asked again.

"There." She stood up and looked down at the funny shape. "It's an arrow so we know how to get to that field again." She paused for a minute, quite proud of her simple but important creation. "Will you come back here with me, James? I need to know what this means."

"Yes, I will," James said. Even though he was scared, he needed to find out, too. He hoped so badly that it had been Zintar. In James's mind, what he'd felt could have been none other than the funny-looking creature who had saved his life and been his best friend. He looked up at Mrs. DuCrét. "Should we go and find him now?" he asked.

"No, James," she answered. "We must get back to town. The sun is setting. It will be dark soon, and I don't know this part of the forest well. But I go for my walk in three days. Will you meet me at the start of the forest path?" The old lady began walking back towards Nemesté.

James hustled to catch up. "Yes, but I have to go to school."

They walked in silence for the next while. James was trying to figure out how he was going to get out of school and into the forest in three days' time.

"James, you run on ahead. I need to wait till it gets dark so I can sneak back to the inn unnoticed," Rionzi said, pausing behind the last tree before the village. "Don't forget, three days." She tugged his arm and drew him close to her.

He could smell the coffee on her breath as he was dragged in close. "I'll be here," he promised, though he still hadn't figured out how. He ran off towards Nemesté.

When James entered the backyard, his mother was outside hanging laundry.

"Where have you been all day?" she asked.

"Just playing in the forest," James answered as he scampered off inside.

Bella stood there for a minute with a worried look on her face. James was back to playing in the woods for days on end. She worried about the crazy stories he might begin telling again. David had told her they should forbid James from playing in the forest, but Bella couldn't allow that to happen. Her son seemed happier when he was allowed to roam freely.

~

The sun was still showing above the mountaintops in the west. The sky glowed pink, and the cool night air was beginning to descend on the village. When the last bit of sun had fallen behind the mountains and the colours faded into dark shades of grey, Rionzi DuCrét began walking back through the village. She tried to hide her face with her scarf in case she came across anyone. She was startled a few times by some cats wandering the streets, but she made it to the inn without being noticed.

She opened the large door and immediately caught Saleem's eye as he looked up from some work at the front desk. She found no words to plead her case but begged with her old eyes for him to pretend not to notice. They both sat for a minute, each holding the other's gaze.

Saleem desperately wanted to know where she had been. He didn't want to get her in trouble, but he was curious. He remembered the old tales of the tree creatures. His dad had told them to him in secret and made Saleem promise to never tell anyone. He had kept his promise and hadn't even mentioned it to Mrs. DuCrét after all these years, but this peculiar behaviour, sneaking in the door after dark when she should've been in the inn, had suddenly sparked curiosity in him.

They still stared deep into each other's eyes, wanting to talk but unable to find the words. There was a deep understanding that Saleem would protect and care for Rionzi DuCrét above all, and she was forever grateful for this.

He finally nodded ever so slightly and returned to his work. She let out a breath, quietly closed the door behind her, and hobbled up the stairs to her musty apartment.

Someone's Watching

Three days later, Rionzi DuCrét went out for her scheduled walk. This time, she didn't need to hide under her scarf or remain in the shadows. The air was crisp, and a light fog lay across the valley. The mountains on the other side could only barely be seen. It almost felt like waking from a peaceful dream. Sunbeams broke through the clouds and made the morning dew sparkle in their light. Rionzi slowly made her way across the village. The few people she did run into avoided her. She could hear the mocking snickers as she passed under the windows of the houses lining the street, but she barely noticed them. She had become accustomed to tuning them out. When she reached the forest, she sat on a large rock and waited for James.

James, meanwhile, had a long walk ahead of him from his school back to Nemesté. His mother had gone with him to the bus, which he would've liked on any other day, but it gave him no opportunity to head into the forest. When he got off the bus at school, he had simply snuck off down a back road that would lead him back to the village, and he hoped his teacher wouldn't call home to ask about his absence. He also hoped that Mrs. DuCrét would wait for him.

As he walked, his thoughts began to swirl over their previous adventure in the forest. The contrast between the kind of fear he had only ever experienced once before with the purple flowers and the excitement he had only ever felt when playing in the forest with Zintar was very heavy on his mind. His feet were getting wet from the dew on the grass as he cut across a cow pasture, but he barely noticed because he was so involved in his thoughts.

James wandered into Nemesté, hoping to go unnoticed. As he passed the inn, he glanced up to the third-floor balcony and was happy to see that Mrs. DuCrét was not in her rocking chair. His pace quickened to a run to get to the forest. As he got to the edge of the village, he stared deep into the trees. He didn't notice the withered old figure sitting on the rock. Rionzi DuCrét woke to the sound of James's little feet scampering along the path. She had dozed off while waiting for her young friend.

Saleem had been peering out the window when James paused in front of the inn to look for Rionzi. He found it suspicious that James had stopped and stared up to the third-floor balcony. The innkeeper had recognized James right away, and a question entered his thoughts: did James and Rionzi DuCrét know each other? It seemed un-likely—but perhaps it wasn't.

In that instant, Saleem made a decision. He grabbed his jacket and began to follow James. He really didn't know why he was doing it, but suddenly he was weaving back and forth between buildings, following the scrawny little boy through the village. He watched as James headed off into the forest, where he knew Rionzi DuCrét would also be waiting.

His suspicions were soon confirmed when an old woman stepped out from behind a tree. He was too far away to see more than a shadow, but he recognized that shadow immediately. He crept a little closer, but there was a bit of an opening before the trees, so he had to remain farther away than he would have liked. From where he was standing, the two shadows, that of Rionzi DuCrét and the little boy, James, stood talking for a minute and then, side by side, wandered down the path into the dark forest.

Saleem didn't know the forest that well. His father had always cautioned him against walking too far. Strange things lurked in the dark shadows, and one could never be too careful. However, it seemed peaceful. A light wind rustled the trees, and small animals scurried about.

James and Rionzi walked along at a moderate pace. They both wanted to get back to the open field, yet they were fearful of what they might encounter. They paused a minute before James noticed the rocks in the shape of an arrow—but something wasn't right.

"Mrs. DuCrét, I don't think that's the right way," he said, pointing in the direction of the arrow. The young boy had a very good sense of direction, and he was sure the right way was more to the left.

"I set this up myself," Mrs. DuCrét protested. She didn't doubt James, but she was confused as to how this could be. Had a few rocks been bumped out of place, she could accuse a deer or a squirrel or some other creature, but the arrow was built exactly the same, just pointing a slightly different direction than James seemed to think it should have been.

"I know, Mrs. DuCrét," James said, confused but insistent, "but I don't recognize that path. I recognize this one."

"Perhaps someone doesn't want us to find that field again," she said, finishing his thought for him.

Saleem stood ten metres back, watching their curious behaviour. He was afraid they were lost.

Unbeknownst to all three, someone else watched each person in the procession. The black eyes of Simputus glared in the cover of shadow, hoping her trick would confuse them.

Suddenly, all at once, James, Rionzi, and Saleem felt a chill overtake them.

"She's near, James," Rionzi said, looking around, trying to see into the shadows. They had both felt this before and knew what it meant, but Saleem was unfamiliar with the sensation. Fear and worry overtook his mind, and he couldn't figure out why. A minute ago, he had only been mildly fearful that they were lost in the forest, but now the fear was much stronger and felt different. It captivated him. It seemed like no matter what he did, he was going to die. He was so afraid that he started walking back to Nemesté.

As he took a quick glance back over his shoulder at the old lady and the boy, he saw a strange shadow cross the path. His panic intensified, but he stood frozen. In the next instant, the fear was gone. *What was that shadow?* he wondered. It didn't look like anything recognizable. His first thought was to turn and run towards the village, but then it occurred to him that whatever that thing was, it seemed to be stalking Mrs. DuCrét and James. Saleem couldn't leave them, but he dared not step any closer just yet.

The Purple Flowers

Simputus saw Saleem turn and head back towards the village. As she crept closer to the other two, she was too focused to realize the innkeeper had stopped.

Meanwhile, James and Rionzi began walking the path that the young boy thought was the way to the field. As they walked along, it became quite familiar to James, and he knew they were going in the right direction.

"Oh, I remember this tree with the funny knot in it," James said. "Oh, yes, and this rock shaped like a house." He got more excited as he recognized each landmark.

Rionzi was amazed at the way the scrawny boy could remember his way around the woods. It all looked brand new to her.

Simputus ran off ahead of them. It was clear to her that they would find the field again. She was determined that it would be the last time they did.

Saleem watched the shady creature disappear in the thick brush. He was amazed at how silently she could walk through the forest. He felt like each step he took echoed through the trees, screaming, "I'm here!" But the odd creature didn't seem to notice.

Saleem only caught a few brief glimpses of the wretched thing. At first he thought she was all black, but a few times, as she crossed a sunny patch that pierced through the canopy, he noticed her legs were deep green and her top was dark purple. Her shape could be described as humanoid: two legs, two arms. But, at the same time, she was nothing like a human. The proportions were all wrong. Her legs were scraggly and skinny, like the stem of a plant, and they even had a few weird leaf-shaped things sticking off them. Her arms were flat and wide, like petals. Everything else about her was sneaky and cunning. She had stuck to the shadows and kept a close eye on

James and Rionzi before running off. Now that Saleem thought about it, it occurred to him that he was doing the same thing, though he was much clumsier about it.

"Mrs. DuCrét," James said as he bounced along, "I don't have that scary feeling anymore."

"You're right," she said. "I don't feel it either. She must not be watching us right now. That worries me a bit."

"Who isn't watching us?" James thought he knew, but he wanted to make sure. "Is it the purple flower lady?"

"I think so, James. Simputus is her name, or at least the name the Fidoris call her by," Rionzi replied.

Saleem followed close enough to hear their conversation now.

The old lady and her young companion approached the opening in the trees where they thought the field was. They slowed their pace. Something wasn't right. The field glowed with a faint purple light.

Rionzi grabbed James's hand to stop him, but he didn't need her to tell him what was covering the field. Just three days before, it had been a lush green field with grass blowing in the wind. Now, purple flowers shot up everywhere. They were mesmerizing. They didn't bend gracefully like the grass but stood straight up, defying the wind.

Saleem crept a little closer and caught a glimpse of the eerie purple field. The flowers captivated him as he began walking forward. The rustling leaves under his feet suddenly caught Rionzi DuCrét's attention, and she turned quickly.

Her first thought was Simputus. Perhaps she had surrounded them. Rionzi was relieved to see the innkeeper. His eyes seemed to stare past her, though. He was walking in a daze towards the purple flowers.

"Saleem!" she yelled and grabbed his arm.

Saleem snapped out of his trancelike state and slowly stared at Rionzi. The rest of their surroundings came into focus as he realized where he was and what he was doing. "How beautiful," he said. "I've never seen anything like it before."

Now that Rionzi had stopped him from advancing towards the field of flowers, she snarled a question at him. "What are you doing here? Are you following me? Do you always follow me?"

Saleem was flustered. He hadn't planned on being seen. "Um, no, I wasn't. Well, I was, but just today."

"Why?" Rionzi asked angrily.

Once Saleem had gathered his wits, he turned the conversation around. "Mrs. DuCrét, with all due respect, you have been acting a bit strange lately. It's my job to look after you and keep an eye on you. I don't think you're dangerous, but the village does, and I have to do my job or we both get punished. You snuck out the other day, and I said nothing. I just let it go. Today, I saw your little friend come looking for you at the inn, and I wanted to confirm a suspicion. That, Mrs. DuCrét, was why I followed you." His voiced rose a little, the same way his father's voice had risen whenever he was worried about his son. "So don't turn this around on me," Saleem said.

Rionzi couldn't argue with the innkeeper. He and his father had been the only people to be kind to her since her return to Nemesté. They had saved her life, though she wasn't sure she always wanted it to have been saved. In fact, many days had gone by when she wished the town had thrown her away. Life was painful and lonely. At least, it had been that way for the past forty years before James came along.

That day not so long ago when the scrawny boy mentioned the Fidoris had brought light back into her darkened heart. The dim hope that she barely held on to had suddenly brightened as they began their strange friendship. Now, what was she going to say to Saleem? She had to tell him something. Could she trust him enough with their secret?

"Saleem, you can't touch those flowers," Rionzi said. "They will kill you." She looked deep into his eyes, wondering whether he would take her seriously.

"Really?" He seemed surprised yet relieved at being warned. "I've never seen anything like them."

"They are mesmerizing, aren't they?" she said.

"Yes. Where do they come from?"

"Someone whose evil gaze is all around us." Rionzi paused a minute.

Saleem held on to every word and hoped for more.

She continued: "They call her Simputus."

"I saw her following you guys. That was why I stayed. What is she?" he asked.

"I'm not exactly sure, but I wouldn't want to get close enough to find out. She's like the embodiment of fear."

Deep in thought, all three of them stared out at the shimmering purple field.

"These purple flowers, though tempting, will kill you," Rionzi said. "That was how my husband truly died, not from his wife going crazy. No doubt you've heard that version of the story."

Saleem smiled a little. "I've heard many versions of the story. My father told me the one about the purple flower. I just didn't know they would be so beautiful."

"Mrs. DuCrét," James, who had been patiently listening, quietly said, "remember what we felt at the other side of the field? How are we going to get there now?"

Rionzi stared contemplatively across the field. "I don't know, James."

"What's on the other side?" Saleem asked.

Rionzi decided to risk telling Saleem of the connection she and James shared. She worried a little that it would put James in danger, but she also mostly trusted Saleem with their secrets. "Saleem," she began, still trying to find the right words, "we believe there may be a Fidori somewhere on the other side." It felt a little strange saying the word aloud to someone other than James. She still said it in a hushed voice, as if afraid it would be heard by the wrong ears.

The word *Fidori* made the innkeeper cringe in fear. "Never allow that word out of your mouth, son," his father had once told him. It was a forbidden word in Nemesté. Anyone caught saying it would be banned from the village. "Fidori..."

Saleem said. "How do you know? I thought they lived on the treetops."

With a smirk on her wrinkly face, Rionzi DuCrét said, "Well, you certainly know a lot about them, considering they're a forbidden subject in our town."

He smiled back at her. "Yes, my father told me about them. They were our little secret. I loved the stories."

She began to explain. "The other day, when James and I were here, we crossed this field. There were no flowers at that time, but Simputus caused us to be overwhelmed with fear. Strangely, we were also filled with unexplainable hope at the same time. That's why we think there's a Fidori over there."

"Why would he be on the ground?" Saleem asked.

"Because he plays games with me," James piped in.

"Saleem, it's a bit of a long story, but James has seen a Fidori, too," Rionzi said. Then she shared the story of how she believed Zintar had come to be on the ground.

Saleem's thoughts raced while she told the story. In all his years, he had never seen such a light in Rionzi DuCrét as he did now. *Is it so bizarre for such a creature to exist?* he wondered.

As the story came to an end, the old lady had an idea. "James, do you know where Zintar got the sap that saved your life?" she urgently asked, her eyes never leaving the field.

"He just had it with him," James said as he rummaged through memories. "Wait! There was one time we drank sap from a little tree. Yes, I remember." The excitement grew in his voice. "It was just a little tree. We sat down after playing a game, and Zintar said that the top of this little bush we were sitting next to looked like a piece of his home. He kept looking at it and finally ripped off a branch and then sucked some sap out. I had some, too. It tasted exactly like the sap he fed me when I almost died. He said it was what he drank at home."

"Do you know where the tree is?" Saleem asked. He understood the plan.

"It was just a little bush, really. It probably got trampled," James explained. "It was years ago."

"Which means it might be bigger, James," Rionzi said. "Don't you see? We could kill the flowers with the sap."

The smile that lit James's face could have been seen for miles. "I think I can find it!" James took off running through the woods.

Rionzi and Saleem followed but were struggling to keep up.

"James! James!" Rionzi yelled as the gap between them grew.

She could faintly hear his squeal through the trees: "I'll bring it back! I'll bring it back!"

After a few more steps, Saleem and Rionzi came to a huffing stop. The two sat for a moment, catching their breath. The uneasy feeling that they had all sensed earlier was suddenly with them again. Rionzi and Saleem glanced at each other with a worried look. Their eyes immediately darted to the surrounding forest, but they couldn't see anything.

"She's here," Rionzi whispered as she took a seat on a large rock.

Before Saleem could respond, the heaviness of their fear was gone. He looked at the old lady, baffled. "Is she gone?"

Still catching her breath, Rionzi coughed before she spoke. "I fear so."

"Fear?" Saleem asked, puzzled.

"I fear she has run after James." Worry dominated Rionzi DuCrét's words. "We shouldn't have left him. We should have stayed together. I should have known. Of course she was near!"

A Grungy Shoe

The place where James remembered seeing the tree wasn't very far. He stood huffing and puffing, looking around for it. Suddenly, he laughed. A beam of light had broken through the canopy and was shining right on the little tree. It was a bit bigger than James remembered, but he was sure it was the same one.

He ripped a branch off, just like Zintar had, and put one of the small cup-shaped leaves underneath the dripping end of the branch. The leaf was full in no time, so he filled up another. When he began to walk away, the sap started splashing out all over his hands, making them rather sticky. After about ten paces, he realized the leaves were now only a sticky mess, and there wasn't much sap in them at all.

"This will never work," he said out loud, frustrated. He walked back to the little tree and stared at it, trying to figure out what to do.

Suddenly, purple flowers rushed through his mind. He stumbled backwards, trying to hide from Simputus's gaze. She was here. As he scrambled away, one of his shoes slipped off, but he was so scared he didn't even realize it until he was hiding behind a big tree, staring back towards the beam of light. His body was trembling, and his big blue eyes darted back and forth, searching for her. He heard rustling from the darkness in front of him.

He could feel her gaze. Every part of his body shook. He closed his eyes. "James, you've got to be brave. There's nothing to fear," he told himself over and over. In a flash, when the overpowering fear from Simputus had eased somewhat, he glanced up and saw the haggard creature wandering to the little tree.

She stopped at his grungy running shoe and stared at it for a minute, walking a circle around it, not letting it out of her sight. James couldn't figure out what she was doing, but then she reached down and put the tip of her green hand inside the shoe. To James's horror, a purple flower grew there instantly.

The unnerving creature stepped back, admiring her work. Suddenly, she jerked forwards as if some invisible force had hit her from behind. It seemed like it was now her turn to be filled with fear. She darted around, trying to fight whatever was making her tremble, but it didn't seem to work. James wasn't entirely sure, but it almost looked as if the tree was getting brighter as she moved closer to it. Simputus looked at the tree and let out a hiss as she slowly backed away into the dark forest.

The smell of the sap seemed to be enough to send her running. When she was gone, James stepped back out and looked at his shoe. The purple flower was wilting away with just the scent of the sap in the air—and that gave him an idea. He used his other shoe and collected as much sap as it would hold.

James quickly headed back to the field. It took a bit longer without shoes, and he stubbed his toe once or twice, but within no time and without mishap, he made it back to where Rionzi and Saleem stood nervously looking down the path. A wave of relief went through them as they saw the young boy bounding through the forest.

"James, why did you take your shoes off?" Rionzi said, scolding almost like a mother.

He was a little out of breath, but he simply set the shoe filled with sap down on the ground to show them. He couldn't help but smile as he did this.

"You got it," Saleem exclaimed.

James nodded proudly.

"Did she come after you?" Rionzi searched his face as she asked the question.

"Yes, she did." He became fidgety as he told the story. "But the tree scared her away."

"James, that's wonderful," Rionzi said. She winked. "You must have been very brave."

Saleem was smiling, too. "And you put the sap in your shoes. However did you think of that?"

The three laughed together. James looked down at his feet. There was a small cut on his big toe, but it was worth it. For a moment, the fear of Simputus's gaze was gone. They relished the peace around them. The field of vibrant purple was oddly beautiful, and they almost hated to have to destroy it.

Mrs. DuCrét found a long stick on the ground and dipped it in one of James's shoes. The thick sap clung to the end and left a sweet smell in the air. She cautiously went towards the field, holding the stick in front of her. The smell was strong enough to wilt the flowers without the sap even touching them.

They had soon made a narrow path through the deadly flowers. Rionzi waved the stick with the sap in front of her, the flowers dying as it passed over them. James picked up the shoe just in case they needed more sap and followed behind. They were all very careful of their steps, not wanting to touch any flowers.

It wasn't long before they were on the other side of the poisoned field. As soon as they stepped out, the hopeful feeling overwhelmed them. James looked at Mrs. DuCrét and smiled. The two of them knew this feeling. It happened whenever they were around a Fidori.

Saleem felt it, too, but not as strongly, because he had never met such a creature. "Where do we go from here?" he asked.

They decided to continue down what looked like a path, and it wasn't long before they came to the entrance of the cave.

Rionzi looked at James. Her old figure seemed to straighten a little. She smiled at him. In the last fifty years, she had never once believed she would actually see a Fidori again. She had hoped she would, but she'd never truly believed it to be possible. "James," she said softly, "I think this is it."

"Me, too," he said, grinning at her.

The Cave

They walked into the blackness of the cave, James bravely leading the way. Rionzi fell in behind, and Saleem came last. When the darkness grew so thick that they couldn't see anything, Rionzi reached forwards and found James's hand, then reached backwards for Saleem's.

The air inside the cave was cool and damp, and every once in a while a drop of water would splat on one of their foreheads. James reached ahead, sliding along the rough sides of the cave. Suddenly, he felt a wall blocking the path. He stopped abruptly, and Rionzi and Saleem both ran into him. They all stumbled a little, but everyone was okay.

"What is it, James?" Mrs. DuCrét whispered.

James felt around. The path still continued, but the opening was only about half the original height. "I think we're going to have to crawl."

"Oh dear," moaned the old lady. "I can't re-member the last time I crawled."

It took her a minute to get down on all fours, but once there she started moving along right behind James. She couldn't help but think how ridiculous they must have looked. A scrawny boy led the crawl, then herself, an ancient woman, and Saleem, a fortysomething man. But all the while she could feel that they were getting closer to what she hoped was a Fidori.

Finally, they reached a part in the tunnel where they could stand up again, and, with a lot of effort, Rionzi and the others were back on their feet.

"There're two different tunnels," James said. All three looked down each tunnel, though it was pointless, because they couldn't see anything.

Then they all saw it at once. It was quite faint, but it looked as though there was a light down the tunnel to the right. It was definitely brighter than the other tunnel, which seemed to lead to nothing but blackness.

"Let's go down that way," James suggested, pointing to the tunnel with the light.

"I agree, James. It can't be much farther now," Rionzi said, feeling stronger already.

The tunnel lit up a bit more with each step, and they could now see one another's outlines quite well. Finally, the tunnel opened up more, and they were standing at the edge of a large, open area.

James was the first to peek around the corner. He drew a deep breath and nearly ran out in the open. Rionzi glanced around before James could take off and held his hand tight.

"James, wait," she said in a loud whisper.

"It's him," he nearly yelled. "It's him, I know it."

"It could be a trap."

Saleem now rounded the corner and saw what they had seen. They all stared for a minute.

"He looks sad and tired and confused," James said, looking at his long-lost friend. "Something's wrong with him."

Rionzi DuCrét agreed. The creature, who they assumed was Zintar, was wandering around in circles. He was stumbling from one edge of the light beam to the other. The Fidori reached cautiously out into the darkness, stared at his arm as if to see the effect the dark had on him, then returned to the light beam. He seemed afraid.

Rionzi pulled James back a bit. "Do you mind if I see him first?"

There was no argument. Rionzi DuCrét walked across the cave, her steps echoing throughout, although she tried to walk quietly. There seemed to be no one else in the cave but the lost Fidori.

As Rionzi got closer, tears welled in her eyes. She could hardly believe her long-lost friend was here in front of her. She squinted a little as she stepped into the beam of light. The long shadow cast over Zintar startled him. He stared at her, and it seemed he recognized her.

"Zintar," Rionzi softly said, "it's me." There was a long pause as they both stared into each other's eyes. All the memories flashed through Rionzi's head, such beautiful moments filled with hope and laughter and love. "Do you remember me?"

He looked at her as if she had come from a distant dream. "You're not her," he mumbled.

Rionzi had a suspicion he meant Simputus. "No, Zintar, I'm not."

"She comes every day to feed me." His words slurred together. His eyelids were half closed. "She leaves a queer feeling, but you don't."

"Mrs. DuCrét," James whispered, his voice echoing in the cave. "Give him some sap. I just know it will work."

Rionzi smiled. "Of course, why didn't I think of that? If Simputus's spell is cast over this entire place, we may all need some soon."

As she looked up from her thoughts, she saw James facing Zintar. They were both staring at each other on the line between the dark and the light. James reached out his dirty little hand, Zintar brought up his four-fingered green one, and they touched. They stood like this for a moment, with little expression on either of their faces. They recognized each other, but at the same time, they both seemed very distant.

Zintar was not his usual chipper, interested, bright self, and James still carried the guilt of not having returned to the forest when he said he would. Even though each had changed a little, they shared a kindred spirit. The touch of each other's hands made their reunion more real.

Rionzi gently took the shoe full of sap out of James's hand. She placed it at Zintar's mouth, and the smell of the sap was enough to give him the strength to take a sip. He took another and then another. With each sip, the fuzziness seemed to leave him. He closed his eyes a minute as he swallowed the sap. When he opened them, a smile lit his face. "Where have you been?" he said as he looked at both James and Rionzi.

James couldn't control himself any longer. He reached out and gave Zintar a huge hug, and they both toppled over. This made them all laugh.

Saleem joined them in the open area. Rionzi still couldn't believe that she was seeing the very

Fidori she thought she had killed all those years ago. For forty years she had been carrying the guilt of her mistake. The guilt was a huge part of who she was, and she wasn't exactly sure what it would be like to live without it. She couldn't quite bring herself to fully embrace Zintar. They had so much to talk about, but she enjoyed watching him and James laughing on the ground. The sap seemed to have worked its magic again.

They had almost completely forgotten that they were still in a cave where Simputus had held Zintar captive when they were suddenly reminded by a gust of wind that brought with it a shadow of fear. It swept in the way a cloud covers the sun and its shadow creeps across the earth. They all felt it at once and grew silent.

Zintar, who had experienced it most fiercely for years on end, began to shake and hide behind James. "She'll be back soon," he said softly.

"How do we get out of here?" Saleem asked. He didn't like the feeling Simputus cast on him.

"Come, follow me. I know a back way out,"

Zintar said with confidence. "Before I got so ill, I walked this way out of the cave."

The caved turned pitch black again, and again they all held hands. The feeling of fear seemed to leave them as they left and retreated further into the cave. It didn't take long before they could see the glow of daylight.

"There, up ahead," Zintar said, pointing. He poked his head out of the little opening first and looked around. Simputus seemed to be nowhere near. They squinted as they exited the cave. Though light had shone into the cave where Zintar had spent much of his time, it felt very different to be outside amidst the green of the forest. The four companions started walking quite quickly towards Nemesté.

Finally, Saleem, who had been straggling behind a bit, stopped them and said, "What are we going to do with Zintar? We can't take him back to the village. They won't let us."

They all stopped. Everyone had been so concerned with getting Zintar out of the cave that they had never considered what they were going to do once they got away.

"But he's real! How can they say no?" James said as he caught his breath. "They can't stop us."

Saleem laughed a bit at James's innocence and ignorance of the situation. "Ha, my boy, you're too young to understand. The people of Nemesté are senseless. They're set in their ways and beliefs, and they won't want you or Mrs. DuCrét changing them, even if you do have proof."

"Saleem, would they really deny the truth after seeing a Fidori?" Rionzi asked.

"Mrs. DuCrét," he said, a bit annoyed, "you are one hundred and fifty years old and they still won't accept that part of your story may be true. No, they wouldn't accept the sight of a Fidori. They'd claim it was a trick, some witchcraft, I'm sure. They don't trust you. No offence, but they think you're crazy, and they're all very unsettled that you haven't died yet. I fear Zintar would only make it worse."

James began to cry. "But we can't just leave him here. She'll come for him!"

"I know, James." Saleem was getting frustrated. "But we can't just march into the village with the creature, either."

"His name is Zintar," James said. He didn't like Saleem calling him the creature.

"Saleem, he can't go home with James. His parents would never allow it," Rionzi argued.

The innkeeper let out a breath. "I know." He stared over at Zintar, who had taken a seat on the ground. He looked tired. Saleem knew he was going to regret what he was about to say. "I guess he'll have to come to the inn for now until we can figure out what to do." He glanced over at the strange creature. He couldn't imagine how anyone could deny he existed, yet he didn't trust that the people of Nemesté were as accepting as he was. He had believed Rionzi all these years. Perhaps that was why it was so easy for him to believe now. It wouldn't be fair to keep Zintar in the old inn for too long, though. He needed to go home.

Rionzi knew this, as well. "Saleem, it can't be long, we know. Zintar"—she looked over at him—"you need to be home."

"I've been searching for home for so long, Mrs. DuCrét. I don't know where to go. There were times in the dark cave when I wondered if home, as I remembered it on the tops of trees, with the endless sky, even existed. Maybe it didn't. Maybe I just dreamed it," Zintar said with a saddened look.

The sun was hanging low in the sky. Rionzi knew they needed to head back to the village. "It's Simputus," she said as she got angrier. "She has a way of making us afraid to believe in what we know to be true. Zintar, you are a Fidori, and there are more and more of your kind on the treetops. I've been there, too. Sometimes I, too, wonder if it was all just a dream, but here you are—and we're going to get you home."

Acknowledgements

First, I would like to thank my good friend Blake Allen. Together, we created the creatures called Fidoris while sitting on the "edge of the hedge" to prune the 15 foot high hedges in our village. I spent many evenings on the balcony of a Swiss chalet, reading each new installment of the story to him by candlelight. I could not have written this story without his imaginative contribution to the creation of the characters. Thank you to Destinée Media for publishing my first book. I am grateful to Ralph and Valerie for their willingness to invest in me as an author. A big thanks to Amanda Kramer Kaczynski for her amazing illustrations! She brought this story to life with her creativity/imagination. Thank you to Devon Brown for the cover design and to Julie Lundy for putting the interior together. There were many people who helped with editing this book. The first read through was done by my Aunt Lin who bravely took the first look. Val McCall from Destinée Media passed along suggestions that helped me as I considered the character development and general flow of the story. I would also like to thank Barb Falk for spending many hours reading through and editing a slightly better version of the story. Jeannie Blair was always there to answer questions, give me an honest opinion, and edit the small odds and ends that needed a sharper eye than mine. Thanks to Talia Leduc for doing the final cover-to-cover edit.

I would also like to thank Miss Blair's Grade 5 class, who became my first young audience to hear the book. They had great questions for me about being a writer and some thoughtful suggestions to help make the story more understandable. Finally, I would like to thank my family. Thank you for reading the story, expressing interest in my writing projects and for encouraging me along the way.

About the Author

Jasmine Fogwell grew up in the small town of Norland, Ontario. She spent many years living in a village in the mountains in Switzerland that inspired *The Fidori Trilogy*. She enjoys skiing, hiking, reading and writing.

About the Illustrator

Amanda Kramer Kaczynski is originally from Eugene, Oregon. She enjoys reading, travel, and meeting new people, as well as making art of many different kinds. She has also lived in the mountains of Switzerland, where she met her husband, Kyle. They live in Madison, Wisconsin

A SNEAK PEAK OF

BOOK 3:
THE JOURNEY TO THE TOP OF THE TREES

A Fidori in Nemesté

Simputus was not far behind the four companions as they crept back into Nemesté. When she returned to the cave and discovered Zintar gone, she had made her way to an opening in the trees that overlooked the village. She had spent many days and nights in this very spot, hating the villagers. They had taken everything that was important to her, and she vowed to haunt them as long as she lived. Now they had done it again by stealing her Fidori. She stroked a purple flower that sprouted up beside her, putting all the poison she could in it as she watched the village sleep peacefully.

Meanwhile, down in Nemesté, Rionzi, James, and Saleem snuck the strange Fidori into the apartment on the third floor of the old inn.

"James, you must go home," Mrs. DuCrét said. "Your parents will be worried sick."

He had skipped school all day, and it was now late in the evening. His parents were probably worrying and might have been searching for hours. He nodded and took off, and as he wandered across the village, lit only by the glow of the streetlights, he was afraid to even imagine what kind of trouble he might be in.

"James!" The familiar voice of his mother rang through the crisp air.

James turned around quickly and waved. He really didn't know what to do, so he smiled and said, "Hi."

She gave him a big hug, and he could tell by her swollen eyes that she had been crying for a long time. "Where have you been?" Her voice was mixed with anger and relief. "When you didn't come home from school, we started to worry. We called the school, and they said you weren't there all day, but I put you on the bus in the morning. Where have you been?" she said again, this time with a bit more anger than concern in her voice.

The longwinded explanation of his mother's worries had given him time to think through his response. He decided he didn't want to lie, but he wasn't going to tell the whole truth, either. He would deal with the punishment he was likely to receive. "Mom, I went to the forest all day," he said. "I'm sorry. I know I shouldn't have, and I should have told you where I was going."

Bella was taken aback a little by his answer. She hadn't been expecting such an honest and apologetic response. She began to weep again. "Oh, James, you shouldn't have gone. We've been worried sick. Why would you do that?"

"I don't know." That part was a lie. "I just did."

His mother had to laugh a little at his stern response. "James, I'm just so relieved you're safe. You'll be punished—you can't run off like that—but I'm so happy you're here." She reached for him and gave him another suffocating hug. His mother's arms wrapped around him were comforting, taking away some of his anxiety about the consequences of his actions.

His father wasn't so warm. "Son," he said sternly when they walked in the door. "Go to your room."

Bella reluctantly let go of James, who silently did as his father had asked. As he wandered up the stairs, he heard the beginnings of an argument between his parents.

"David, really, you could have acted a bit more relieved to see him," Bella argued.

"Bella, I am relieved, but he needs to understand the severity of pulling a stunt like that. He can't just wander off into the forest to play with imaginary friends while we have half the village worrying about him."

Their conversation went on for over an hour. James quietly shut his door so he didn't have to listen to it. He knew what he had done seemed wrong to them, and they had every right to be angry, but they didn't understand. It was confusing for him because he didn't know how to make them understand without telling them about Zintar, and he couldn't bring himself to do that. He didn't trust them enough. They probably wouldn't believe him, anyway, just as they hadn't before. There was too much at risk now if he said anything.

A light tap on his bedroom door startled him out of his thinking.

"James." His father's stern voice came through the door, though it had softened a bit since he had first come home. "Would you come downstairs, please? Your mother and I would like to speak with you."

"Yes, Father, I'll be right down." James waited till he heard his father reach the last step. Then he made his way down to the living room to accept his punishment.

Two lamps lit the room with a pleasant glow. David sat in one chair, and Bella sat on the long couch. He could feel their eyes glaring at him before he looked up. When he finally caught a glimpse of both their faces, he realized they had both been crying. He was a little surprised, because his dad had been so angry, but when he looked again to see, he was pretty certain his eyes were red and swollen. There was also a pile of tissues overfilling the waste basket. James wanted to cry, too, knowing he had caused his parents so much grief, but he held back because he knew he had to be brave in facing his punishment.

"James, I'm not sure where to start." David broke the awkward silence. "Your mother and I are very shaken up over what happened today. Do you have anything you'd like to say?"

"I shouldn't have done it," James muttered meekly.

"Then why did you?" David asked.

"I don't know," James lied.

"James, you understand you can't disappear like that without some consequences?" His father seemed to be asking for some sort of explanation.

"Yes, sir" was all James said.

"If you don't have anything else to say, your mother and I have decided to ground you from the forest for a month."

James couldn't hold his tears back any longer. "Yes, sir," he said with a sniffle.

His father's voice began to shake. "James, we would be bad parents if we just let it go."

All three were crying a little, looking down and trying to hold back tears.

"You can go now," his father said before getting up and leaving the room.

James went up to his room and cried for a long time. He was glad it was over. He felt a little bit guilty for lying to his parents, but he didn't trust them enough to tell them about finding Zintar. He was exhausted from the long day, and it didn't take long for him to drift off to sleep.

To find out what happens to James, Rionzi and Zintar, be sure to read The Journey to the Top of the Trees, Book 3 of The Fidori Trilogy!

Lightning Source UK Ltd.
Milton Keynes UK
UKOW05f0601240617
303985UK00001B/13/P